DreamWorks

GABBY'S DOLLHOUSE

A FAiRY-Tastic SLEEPOVER

KU-338-219

ORCHARD BOOKS

First published in Great Britain in 2023 by Hodder & Stoughton

DreamWorks Gabby's Dollhouse © 2023 DreamWorks Animation LLC. All Rights Reserved

A CIP catalogue record for this book is available from the British Library

ISBN 978 1 40837 054 4

1 3 5 7 9 10 8 6 4 2

Printed and bound in China

Orchard Books
An imprint of Hachette Children's Group
part of Hodder & Stoughton Limited
Carmelite House
50 Victoria Embankment
London EC4Y 0DZ
An Hachette UK Company
www.hachette.co.uk
www.hachettechildrens.co.uk

THIS BOOK BELONGS TO:

_____

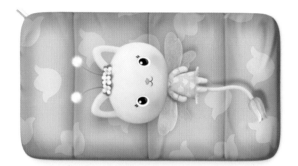

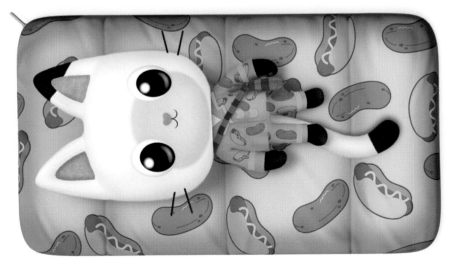

Gabby and Floyd were getting ready for bed. She was just about to tuck him in with his favourite toy mouse when she heard some familiar musical meows. "Do you know what that sound means? It's time for a Dollhouse Delivery!"

Dollhouse Delivery! What could it be?

"Let's see what we have in the Meow Meow Mailbox today! Wow, it's a Kitty Fairy box!"

Inside the box, Gabby found a tiny little sleeping bag, a tiny little pillow and tiny little kitty slippers. "Hey, these are all things you'd take to a sleepover... we're gonna have a sleepover in Kitty Fairy's garden!"

Gabby headed to the dollhouse. "Check out the Fairy Tail Garden. Look how sparkly and twinkly it is!"

Time to get tiny! With a little magic, Gabby and Pandy Paws shrunk and found themselves inside the dollhouse.

"Welcome to the Fairy Tail Garden!" Gabby announced.

"Hey, Pandy. Hey, Gabby," said Kitty Fairy, as she flew over to greet them.

"We're so excited about the sleepover!" Gabby told her.

"Me too. It's gonna be fairy-rific!" said Kitty Fairy.

Pillow Cat rolled over with Baby Blossom. "I just read this guy a bedtime story," she said. "Now he's ready to snuggle up!"

"Oh, thank you, Pillow Cat. Are you going to join us for the sleepover?" asked Kitty Fairy.

"Oh, um … I'd love to, but … I just can't," she said nervously.

"Is something wrong, Pillow Cat?" Gabby asked.

"No, it's just … OK, I've never been to a Kitty Fairy Sleepover before. I don't know what it'll be like," she said.

"You know what? Neither have we," Gabby said. "What if we all give it a go together?"

"OK, I'll give it a try," said Pillow Cat.

"I like your cat-titude!" Gabby told her with a hug.

"Let's get this sleepover
party started!" said Kitty Fairy. "First thing's
first – you three need some pyjamas."
"But I didn't bring any," said Pillow Cat.
"Not a problem," said Kitty Fairy. "Come this way!"
Kitty Fairy led them to a tall tree. "When it's time for pyjamas
at a Kitty Fairy Sleepover, all you need to do is pick some!"
"Whoa! Pyjamas grow on trees?" asked Pandy Paws.

Gabby picked out the pink heart pyjamas and Pillow Cat chose a nightgown with stars and moons on it. Pandy Paws spotted a pair with hot dogs and pickles on them.

"Those are definitely for me!" he said.

"Now that we all have our pyjamas on, it's time for a special Kitty Fairy Sleepover snack. Follow me!" said Kitty Fairy.

Kitty Fairy led them through the garden, over a bridge and to a tree stump. "Our special snacks are right through that door!" she said.

"Hmm ... that door looks pretty small," said Pandy Paws, "but if our special snack is inside, I'll give it a shot!"

"Don't worry, Pandy," said Kitty Fairy with a laugh. "All we need is a little garden magic!"

Kitty Fairy used her magic to make everyone even smaller.

"Are you kitten me!? We are so tiny!" exclaimed Pandy Paws.

"Sleepovers are full of magical surprises!" said Kitty Fairy. "Now we're all small enough to fit through the door."

"But how are we going to get up there?" Gabby asked.

"By using your fairy wings, of course!" giggled Kitty Fairy, as wings magically appeared on her guests.

Gabby, Pandy Paws and Pillow Cat used their new fairy wings to fly up to the door.

"So magical!" said Pillow Cat once they got inside.

The friends flew past fairy-rific flowers, paw-some plants, green grass and a rushing rainbow river!

"Welcome to Fizzy Fairy Juice Falls," said Kitty Fairy.

"Can we drink Fizzy Fairy Juice?" asked Pandy Paws.
"Of course," said Kitty Fairy. "But to drink it, you need a very special fairy cup – a flower cup!"

They each plucked a flower cup, filled it with Fizzy Fairy
Juice and sat down to a fancy, fairy-tastic tea party!
"Now, who's up for a snack?" asked Kitty Fairy.

Kitty Fairy handed out purple popcorn boxes to all of her guests.
"Uh, Kitty Fairy ... there's no popcorn in here," said Pillow Cat.
"There will be! Rainbow Fairy Popcorn is always best when it's freshly popped. Get ready!" said Kitty Fairy, as she waved her tail past the Rainbow Corn.

"It's raining popcorn!" Gabby said, as
they all flew around filling their boxes.
"Delicious!" said Pandy Paws.
"I've had popcorn before, but never like
this," said Pillow Cat.

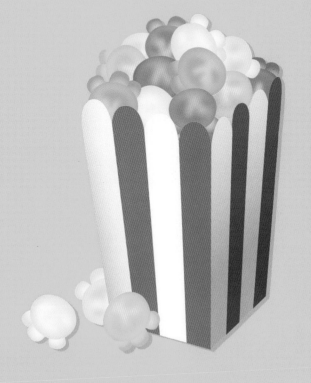

"Mmmm, I knew I smelled popcorn," said a giant CatRat.

"Hi, CatRat! You're SO big," Gabby giggled.

"I'm just my normal size. You guys are all tiny!" he laughed.

"CatRat, would you like some popcorn?" asked Kitty Fairy.

"Don't mind if I do! Thanks, Kitty Fairy," said CatRat as he popped some into his mouth. "Bye, tiny friends!"

"Are you glad you stayed for the sleepover?" Gabby asked Pillow Cat.

"Of course!" she told Gabby. "Thank you for helping me try something new. We're having the best, most magical Kitty Fairy Sleepover ever! I dream about a lot of amazing things, but I never thought a Kitty Fairy Sleepover would be like this. What's next?"

"Ooh, let's see," said Kitty Fairy, as she checked her schedule. "Pyjama tree, fairy wings, fairy snacks. Ooh, it's time for Starry Story Time!"

"That sounds a-meowzing!" said Pandy Paws.

"I think you're going to love it! Let's go back to our sleeping spot," said Kitty Fairy.

"Now, before we snuggle up for Starry Story Time, we have to brush our teeth," said Kitty Fairy.

"Uh-oh, I didn't bring my toothbrush," said Pandy Paws.

"Pandy, it's a Kitty Fairy Sleepover. I have everything you could ever need," Kitty Fairy told him. She pointed her tail at a nearby bush and four toothbrushes with tiny wings flew over to them. "Even brushing your teeth is magical at a Kitty Fairy Sleepover!" said Pillow Cat.

"OK, everyone," said Kitty Fairy. "Get comfy, lay back on your sleeping bag and look up at the stars."

"They're so sparkly," Gabby said.

"They're so beautiful," said Pandy Paws.

"At Starry Story Time, we look for shapes in the stars and then use those shapes to tell a story," explained Kitty Fairy.

"Pillow Cat, do you see any shapes in the stars?"

Pillow Cat saw a big, squishy pillow planet.

Gabby saw a Pandy Paws.

And Pandy Paws saw a surfboard.

"Now we get to tell a story with the shapes we saw," said Kitty Fairy.

"Pillow Cat, do you want to tell the story?" asked Kitty Fairy.
"I'd love to!" she said.

"Once upon a time ... Pandy jumped on a surfboard and surfed the stars. He surfed over the Pegasus and under the North Star. Then he surfed until he reached the pillow planet."

"He was so tired from all that star surfing that he fell fast asleep and he had the most wonderful dream…" finished Pillow Cat.

"About pickles and hot dogs!" added Pandy Paws.

"I don't want this Kitty Fairy Sleepover to end!" said
Pillow Cat. "I'm so glad I tried something new."
"Me too," Gabby said with a smile.

Are you ready for a surprise?
You get to pick the Gabby Cat of the Day!
Choose a Gabby Cat and make up a song for them.